How to take care of Snake Bites

Mary Engrav, MD

Dedication

To the children and adults who may read this book: Truly believe in yourself and your own superpowers. You are a one-of-a-kind person, and your friendly smile and kind words can change someone else's life forever.

Acknowledgement:

Thank you to my family for helping me continue to grow, and for helping me see the world in a different and more beautiful way.

About the Author

The author, Mary Beth Engrav MD, is a mother and grandmother who lives in Portland, Oregon.

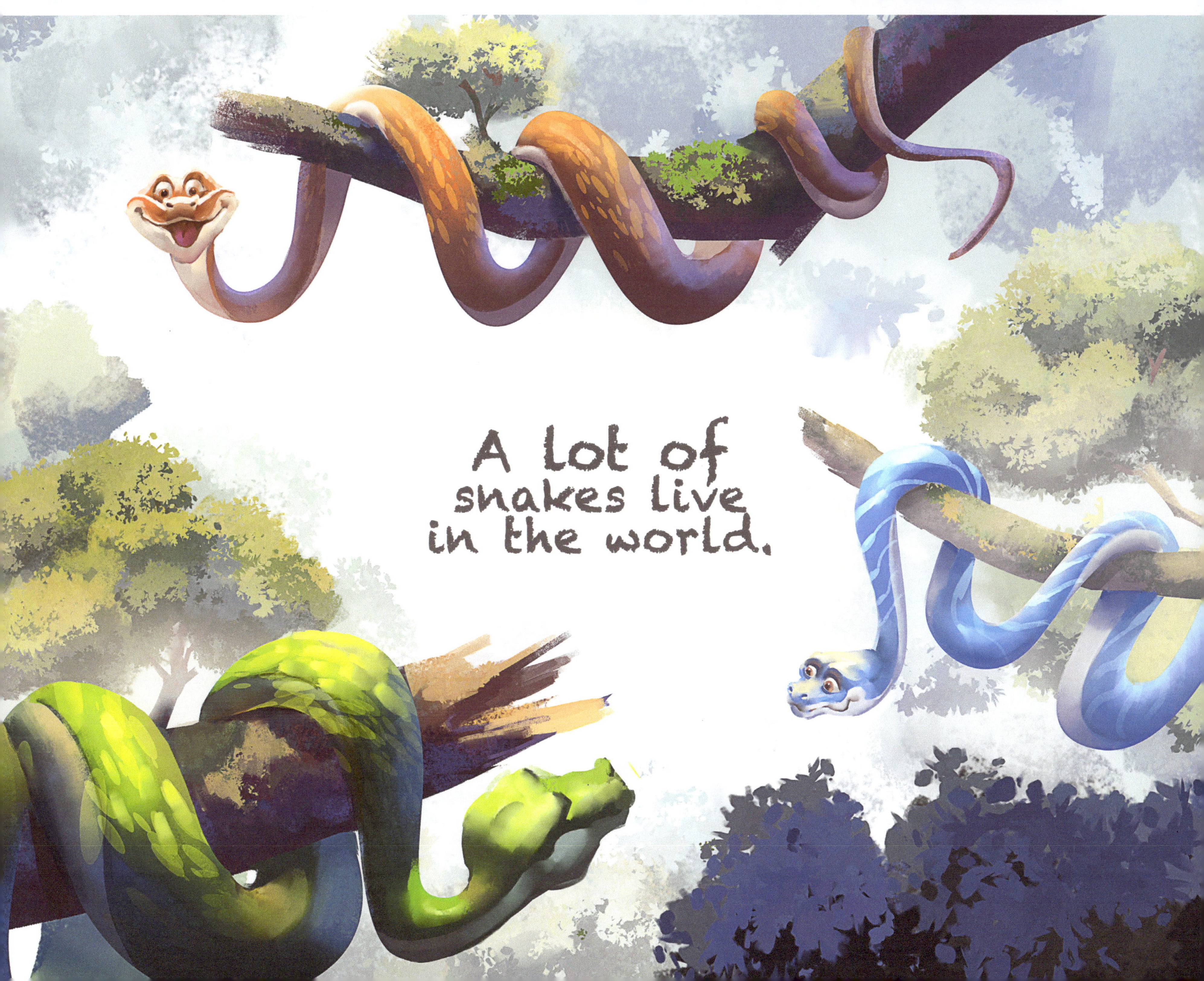

A lot of snakes live in the world.

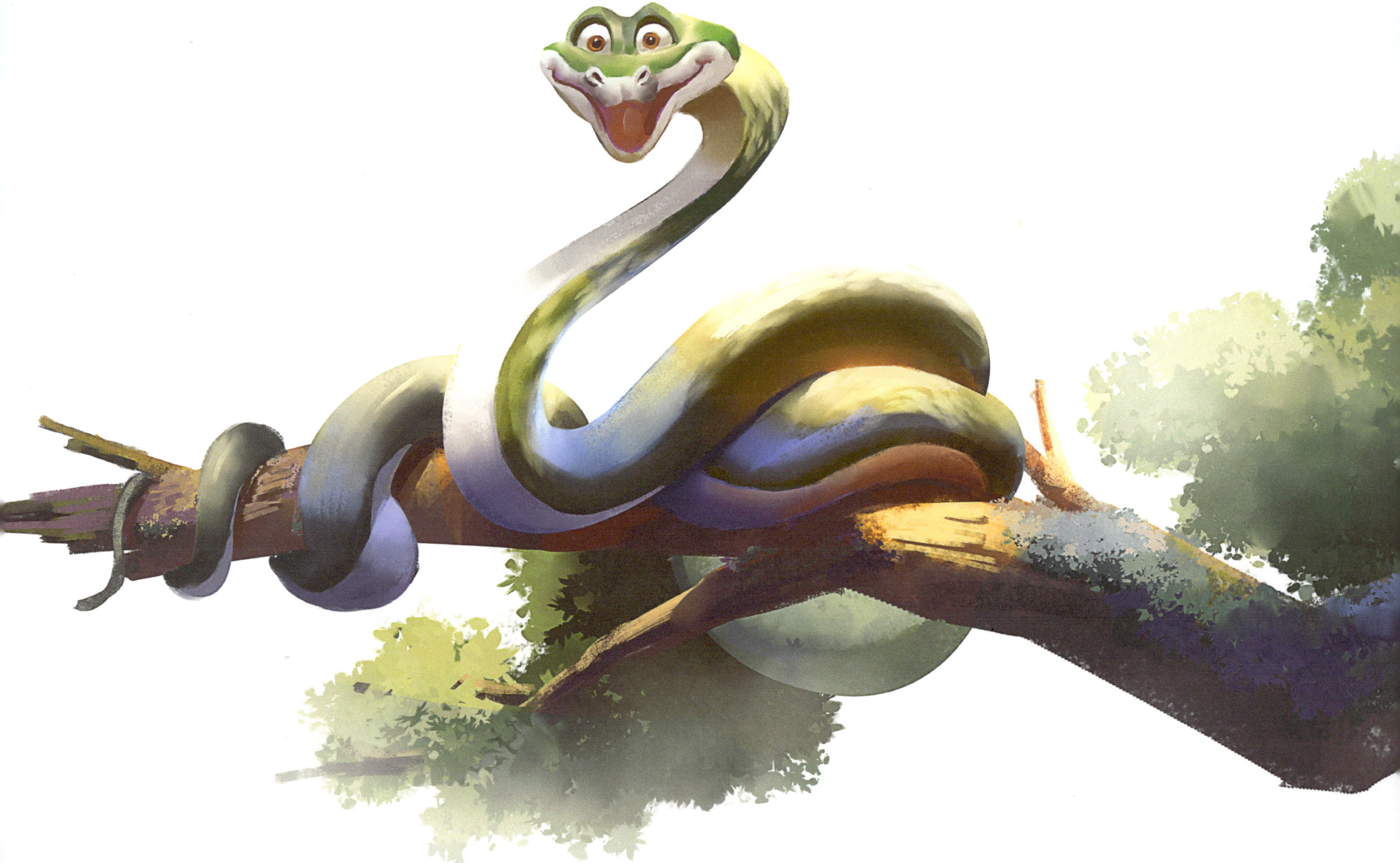

Some snakes are nice.

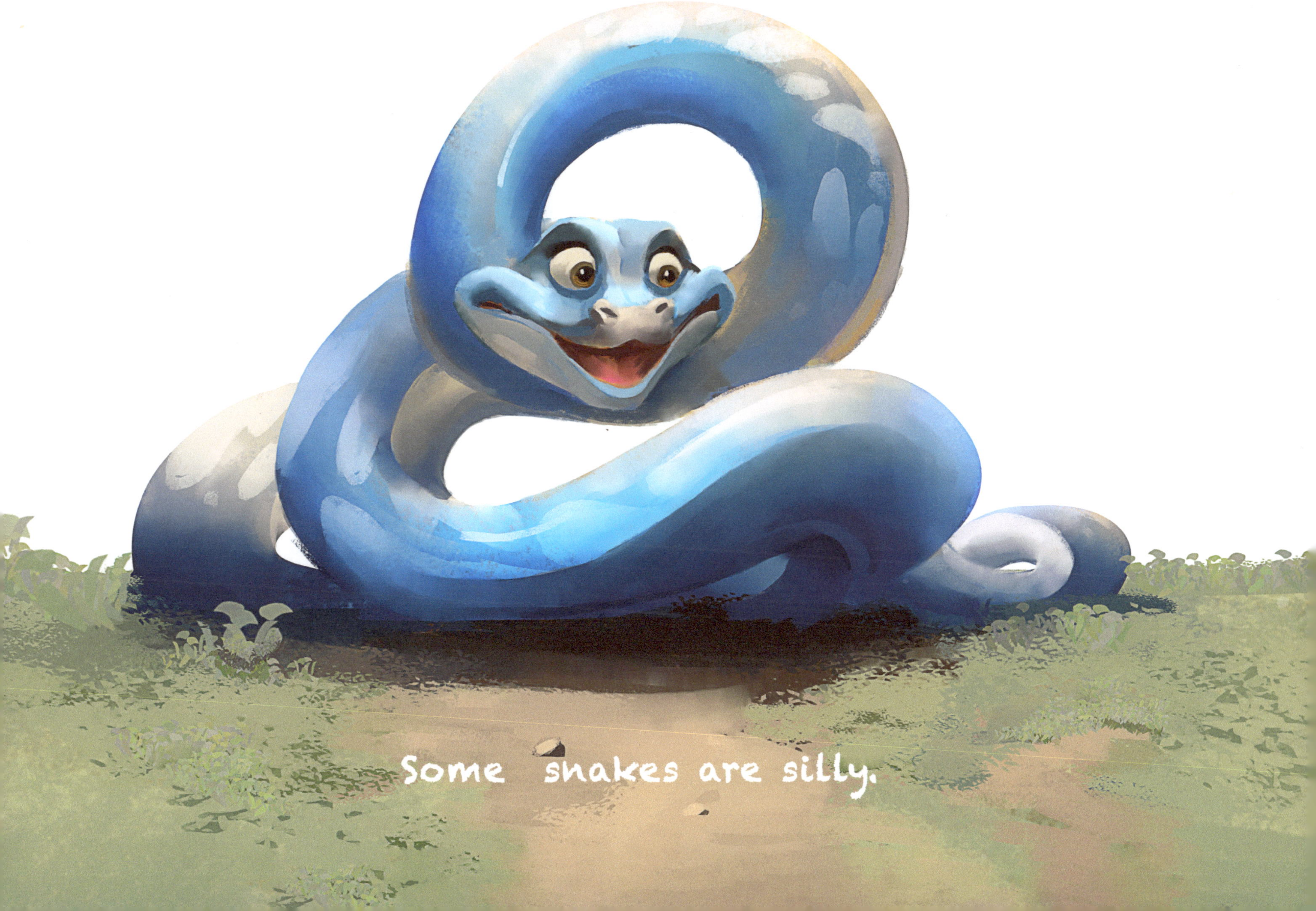

Some snakes are silly.

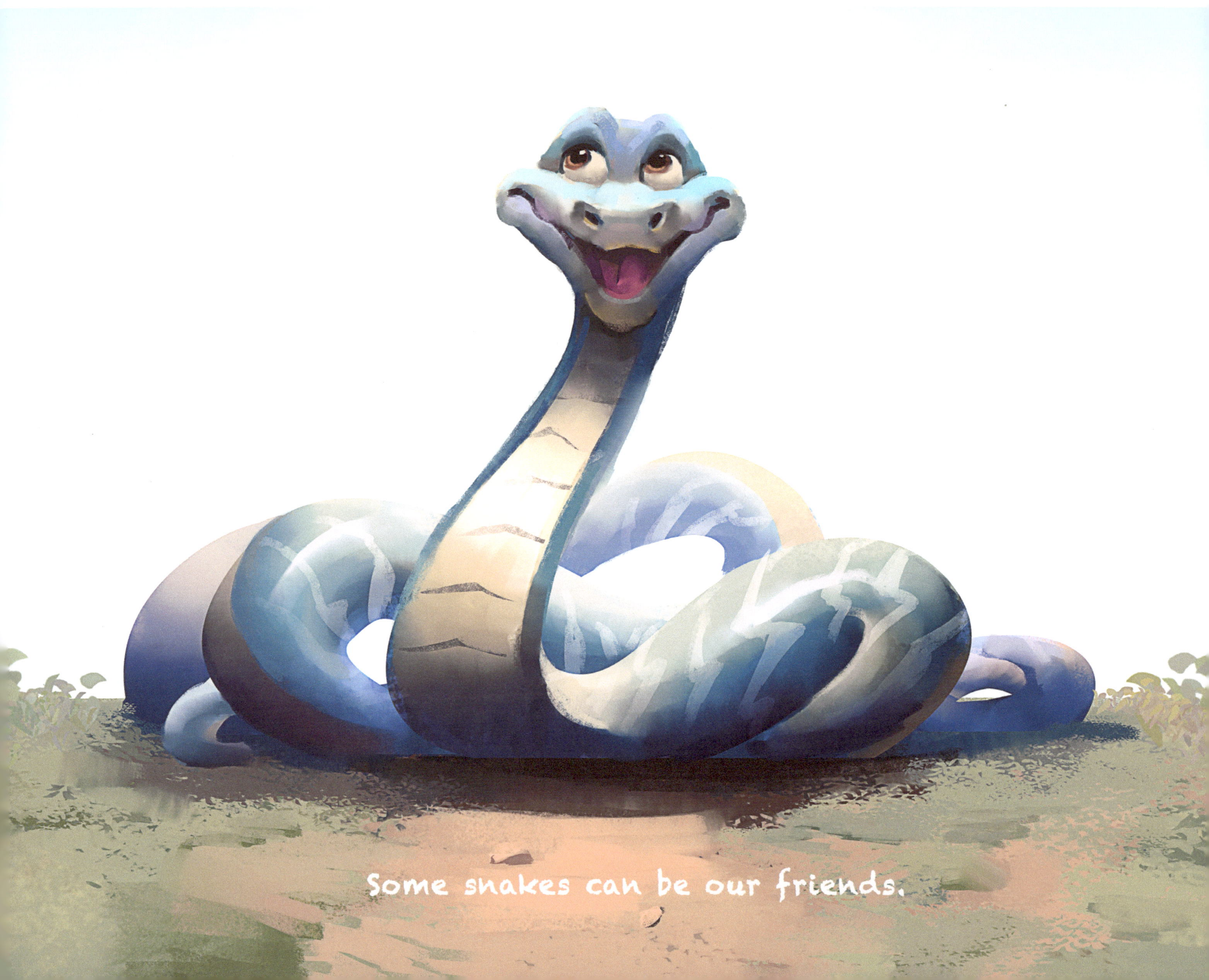

Some snakes can be our friends.

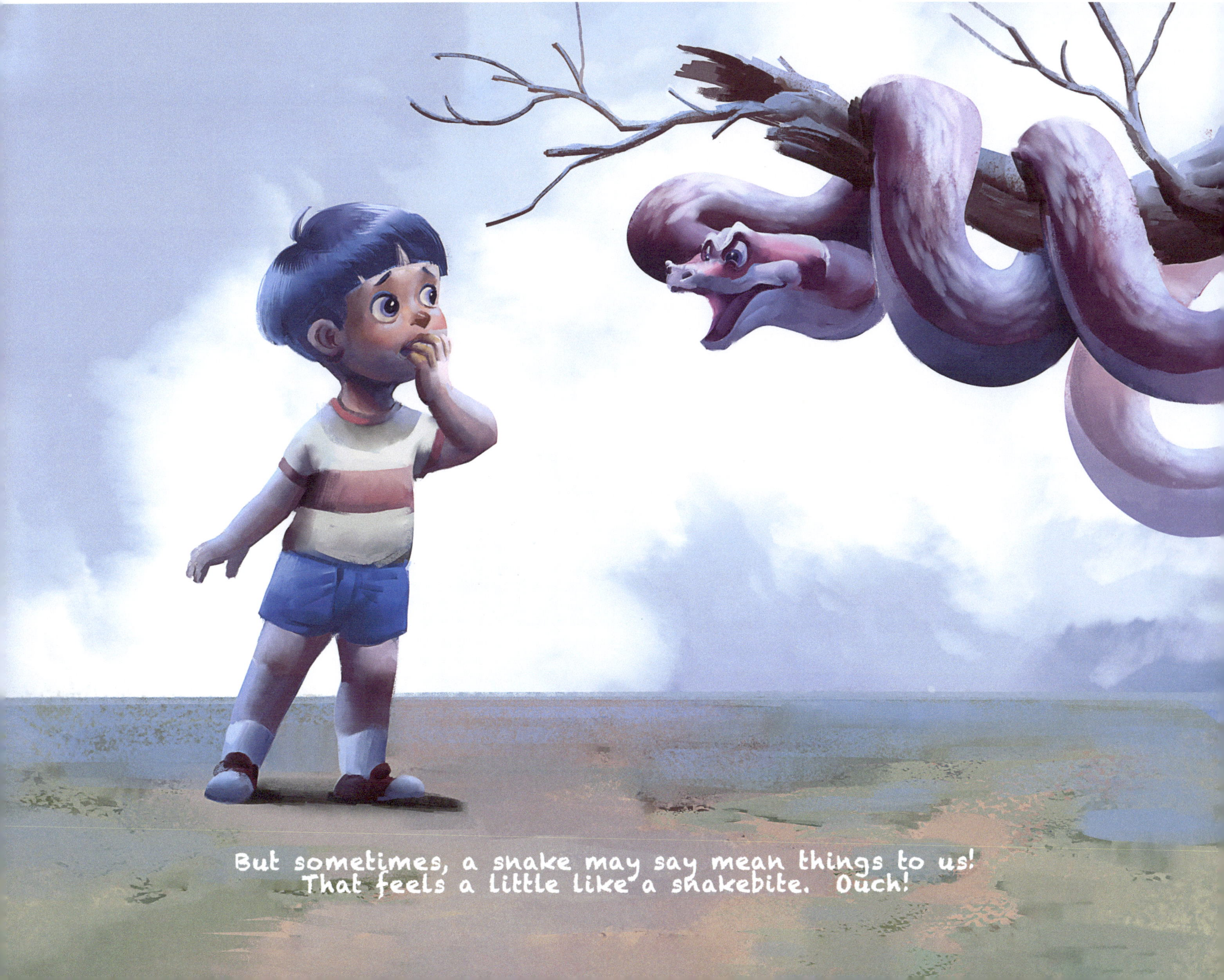

But sometimes, a snake may say mean things to us!
That feels a little like a snakebite. Ouch!

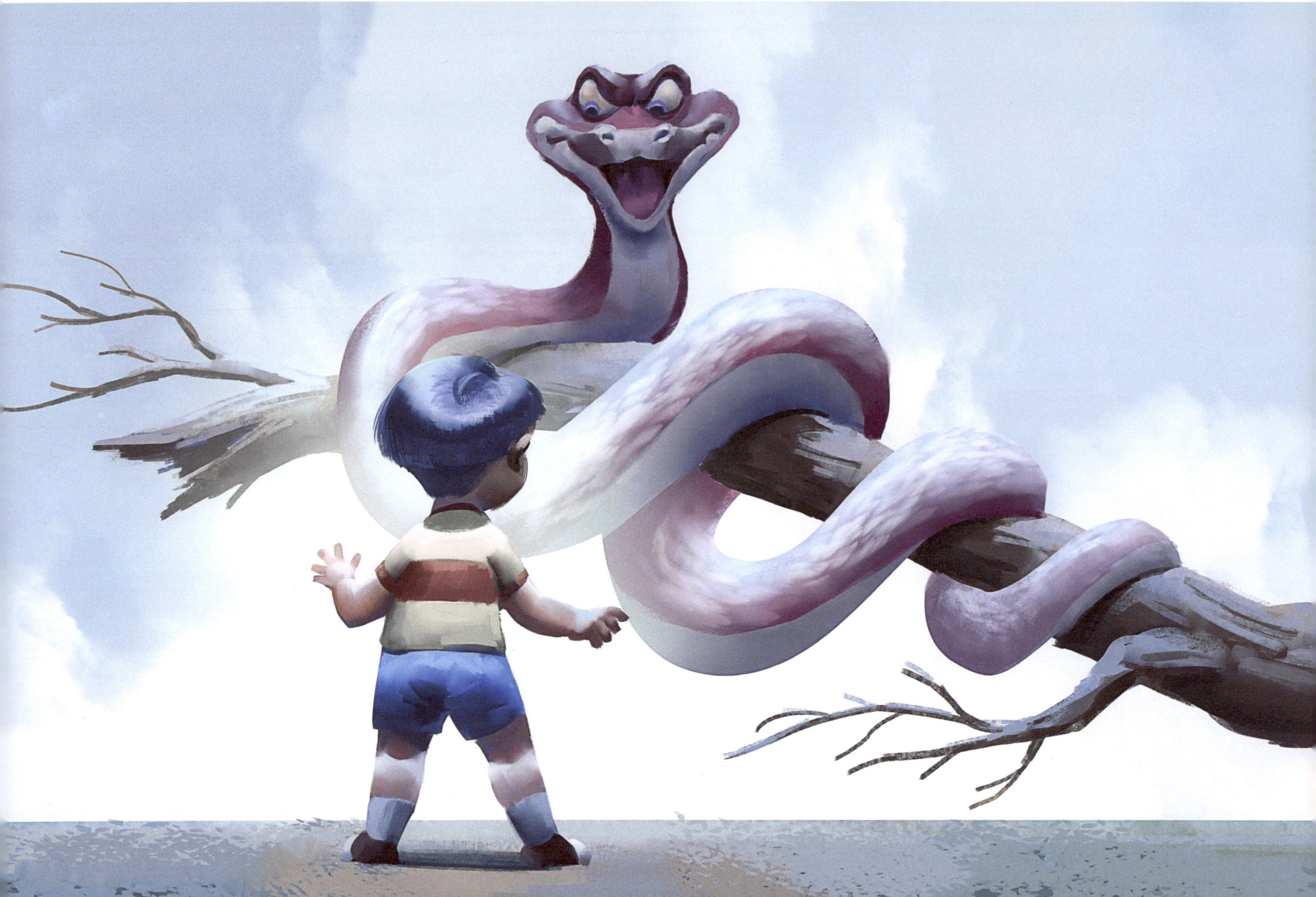

What can you do to protect yourself from mean words, and from snakes who are acting like a bully?

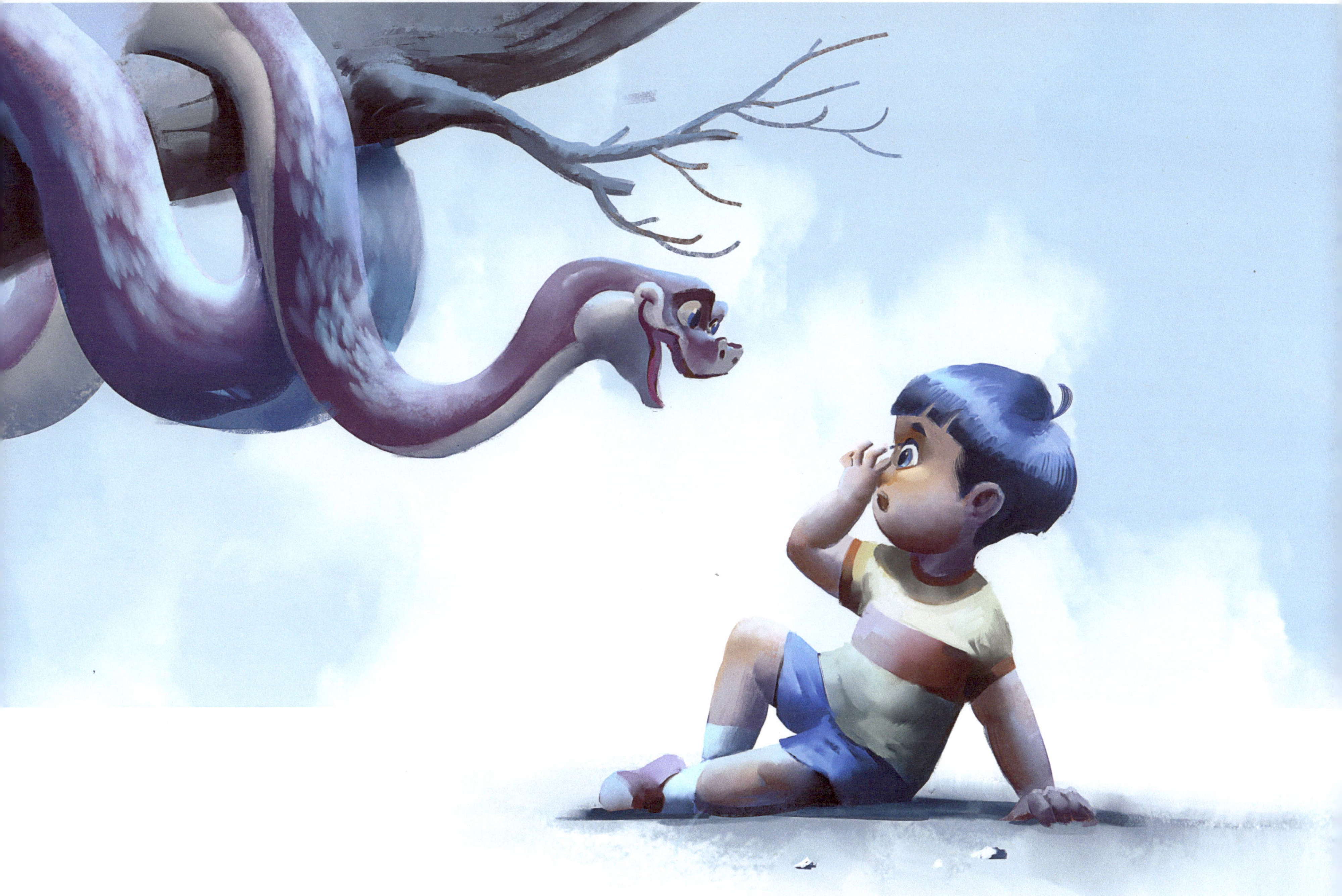

You can carry a pretend snakebite kit, filled with ways to treat those little bites. But what should you put in your snakebite kit?

You can carry a little plan to try and IGNORE the snake. If you ignore a snake that is being mean, sometimes it will go find something else to do. Take some deep breaths, think of something happy, ignore the snake's mean words, and the snake may go away.

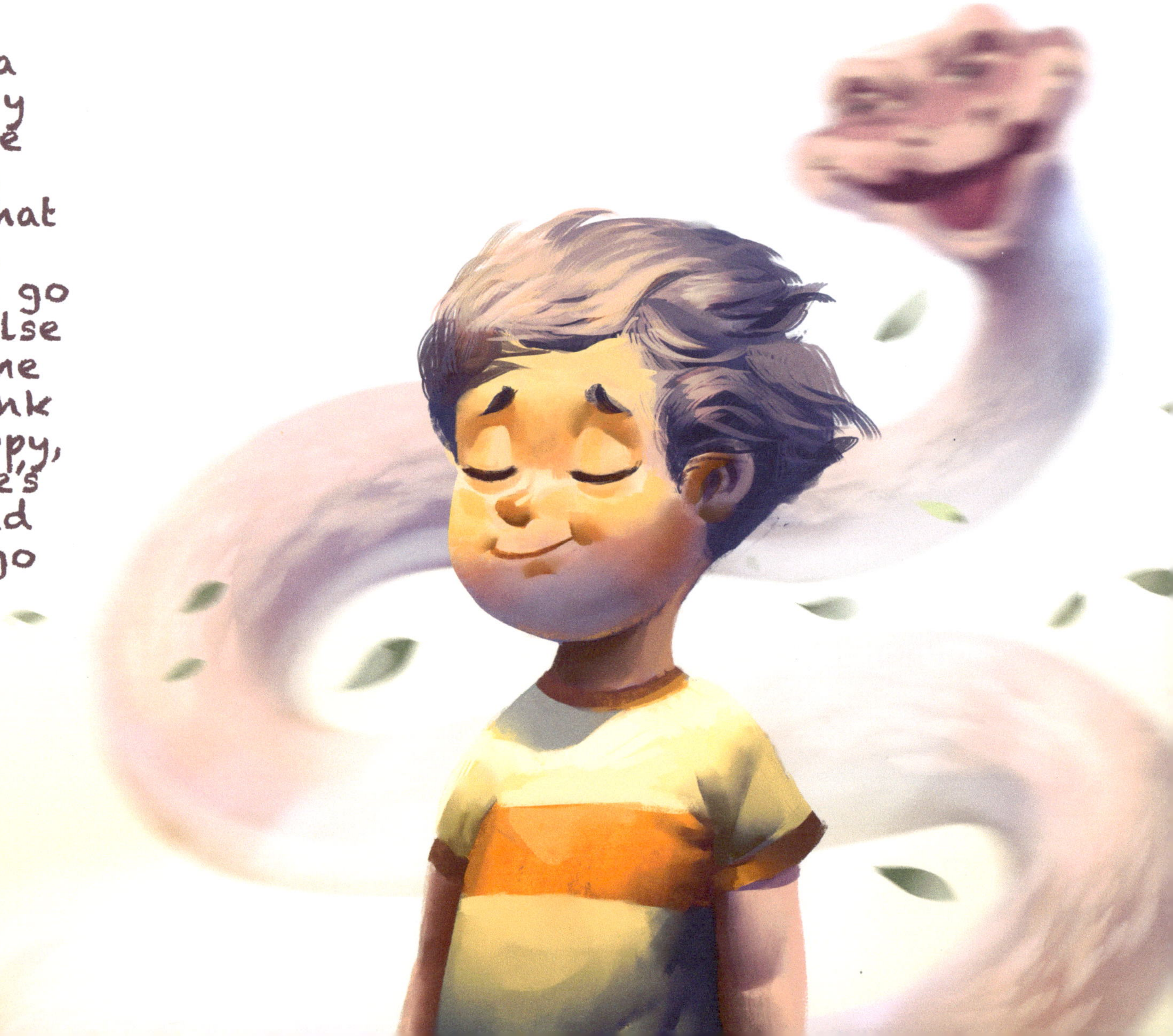

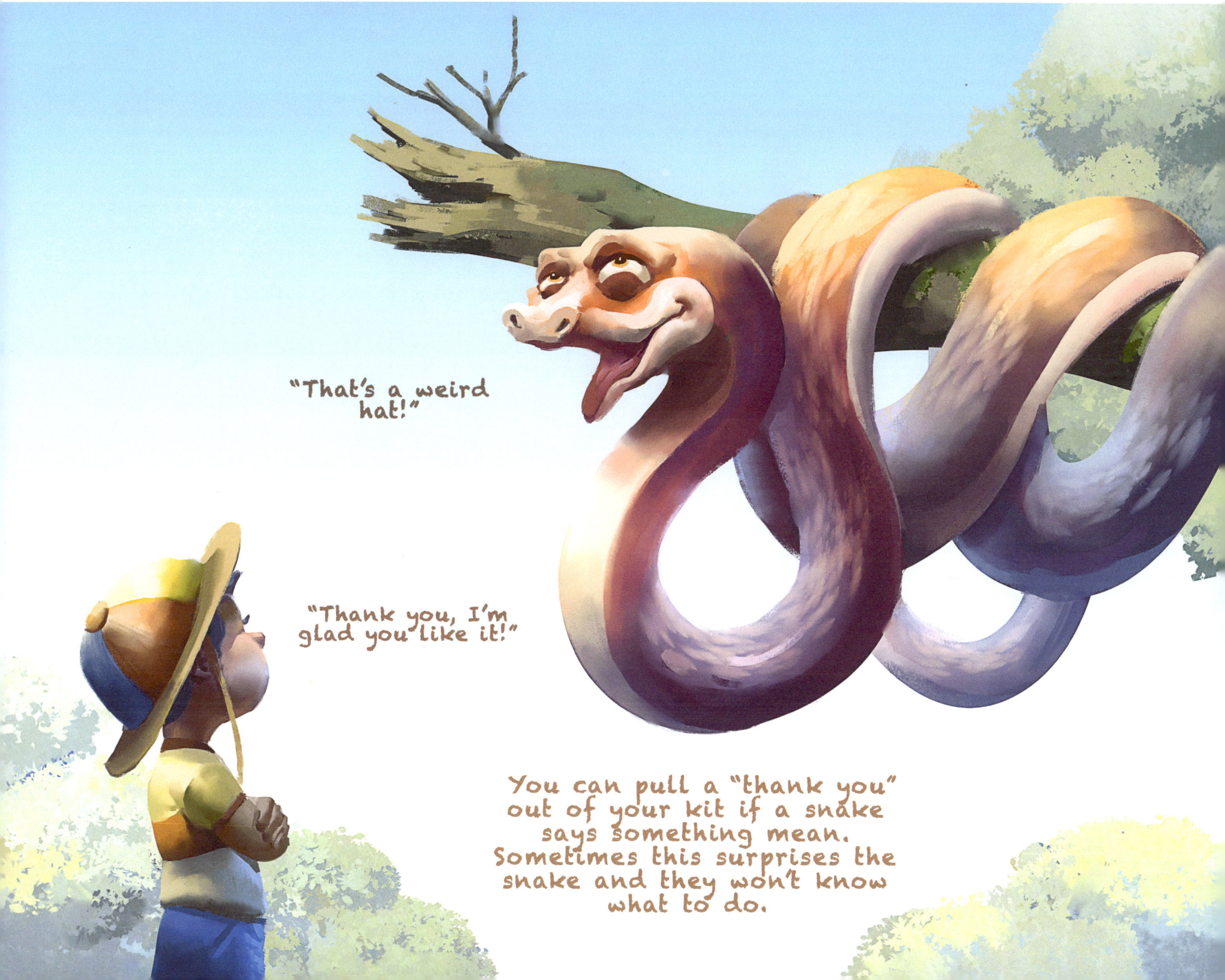
"That's a weird hat!"
"Thank you, I'm glad you like it!"

You can pull a "thank you" out of your kit if a snake says something mean. Sometimes this surprises the snake and they won't know what to do.

You can carry your very favorite things in your snakebite kit! Things that make you happy, no matter what anyone else says.

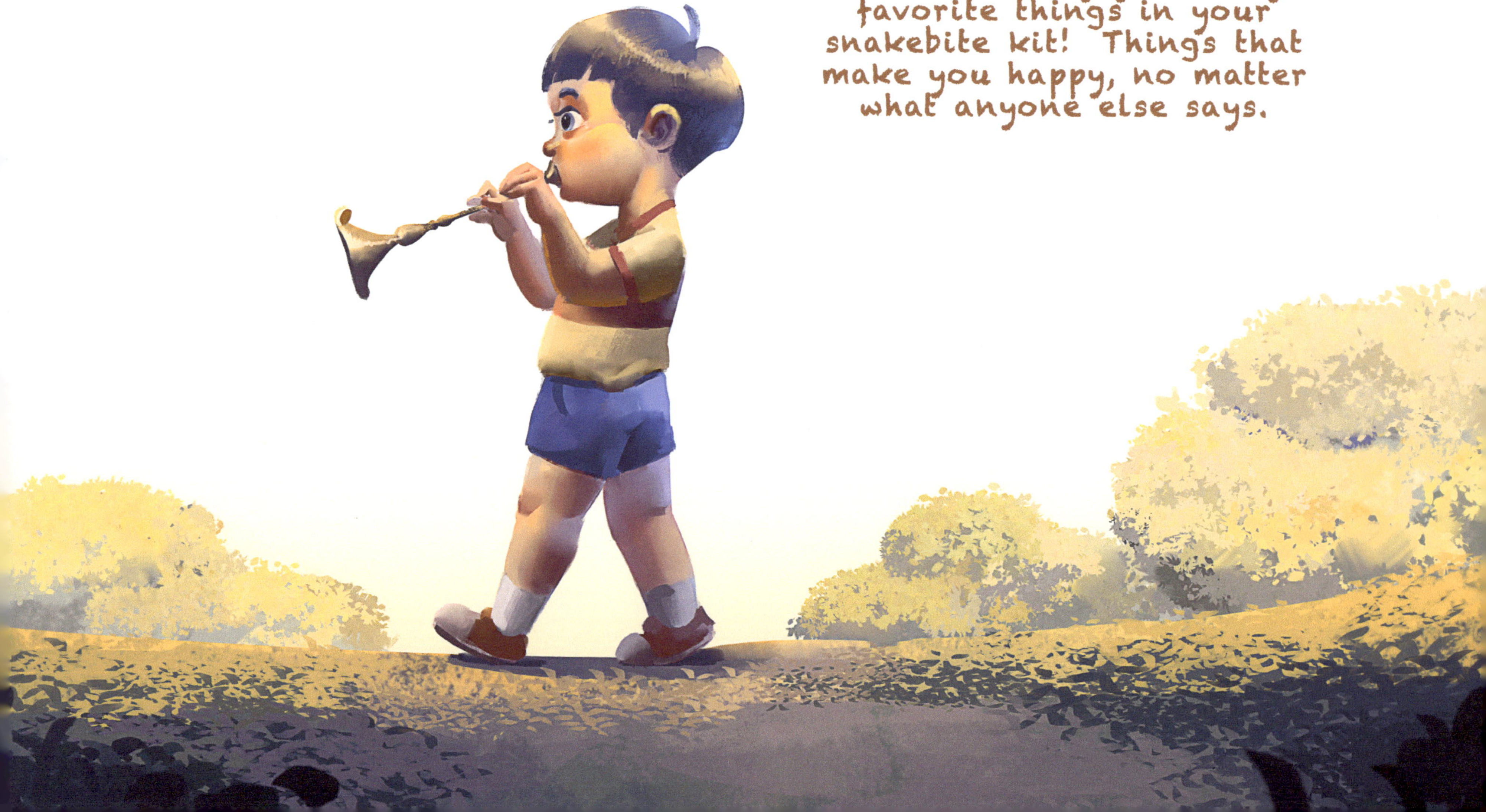

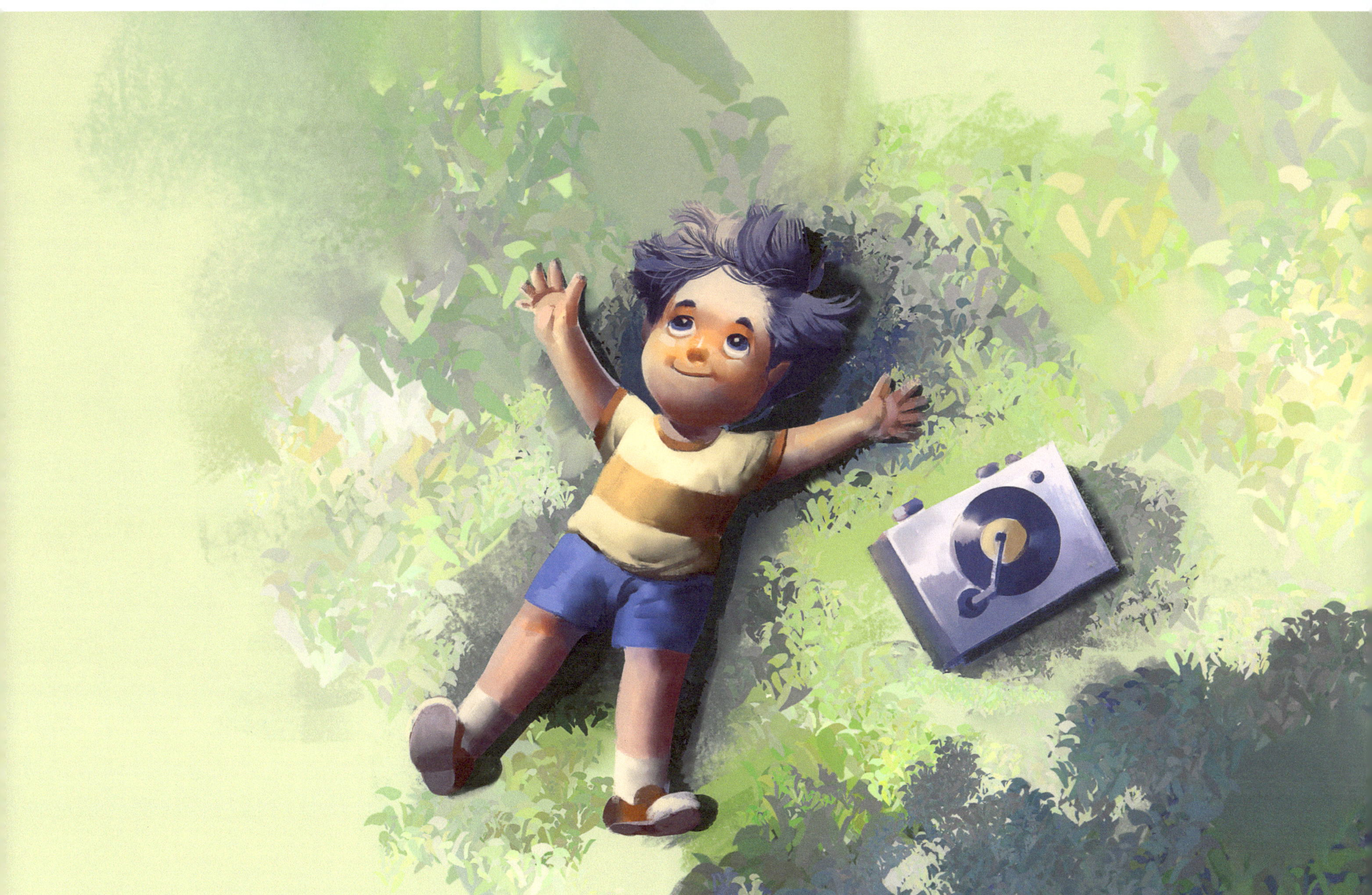

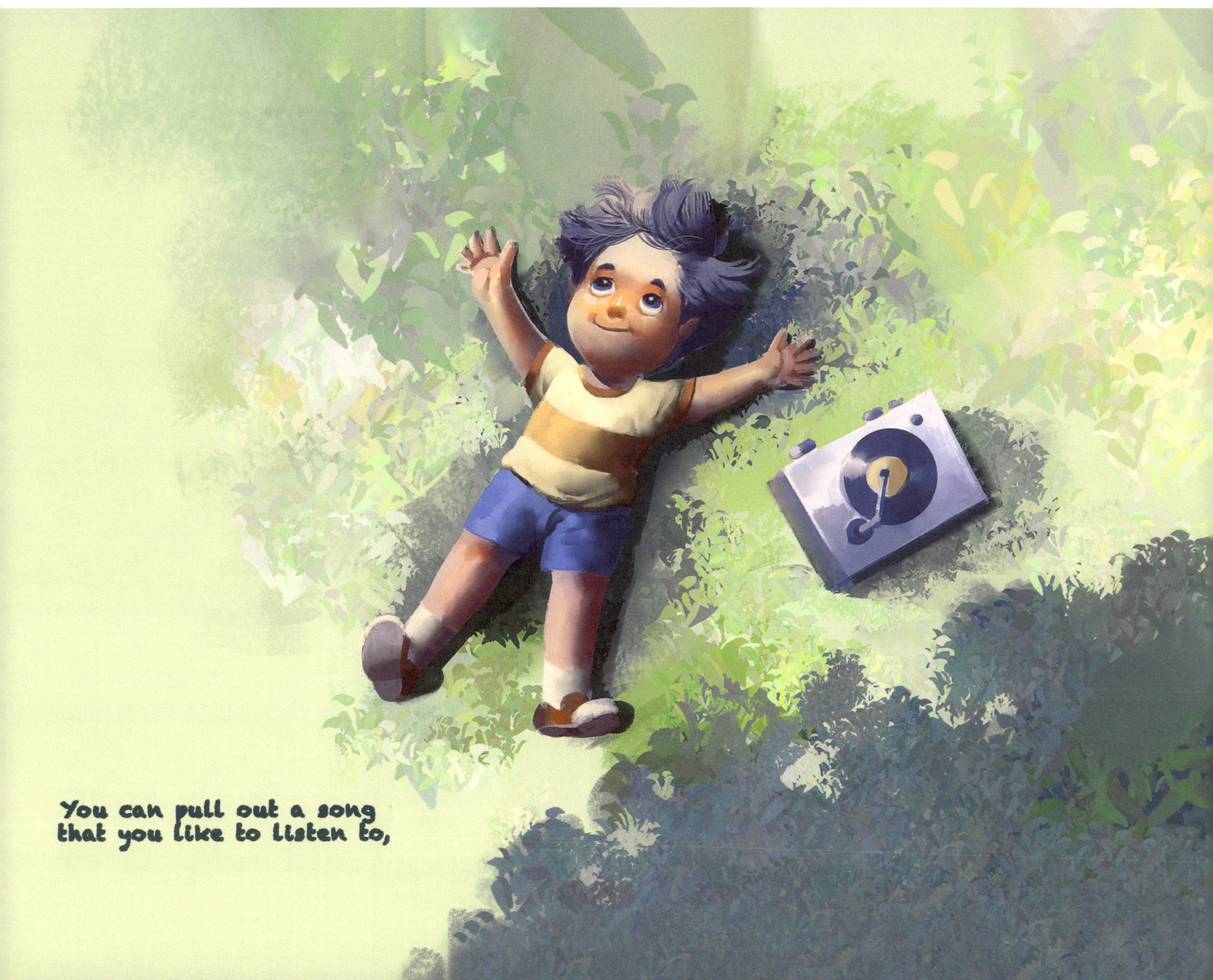

You can pull out a song
that you like to listen to,

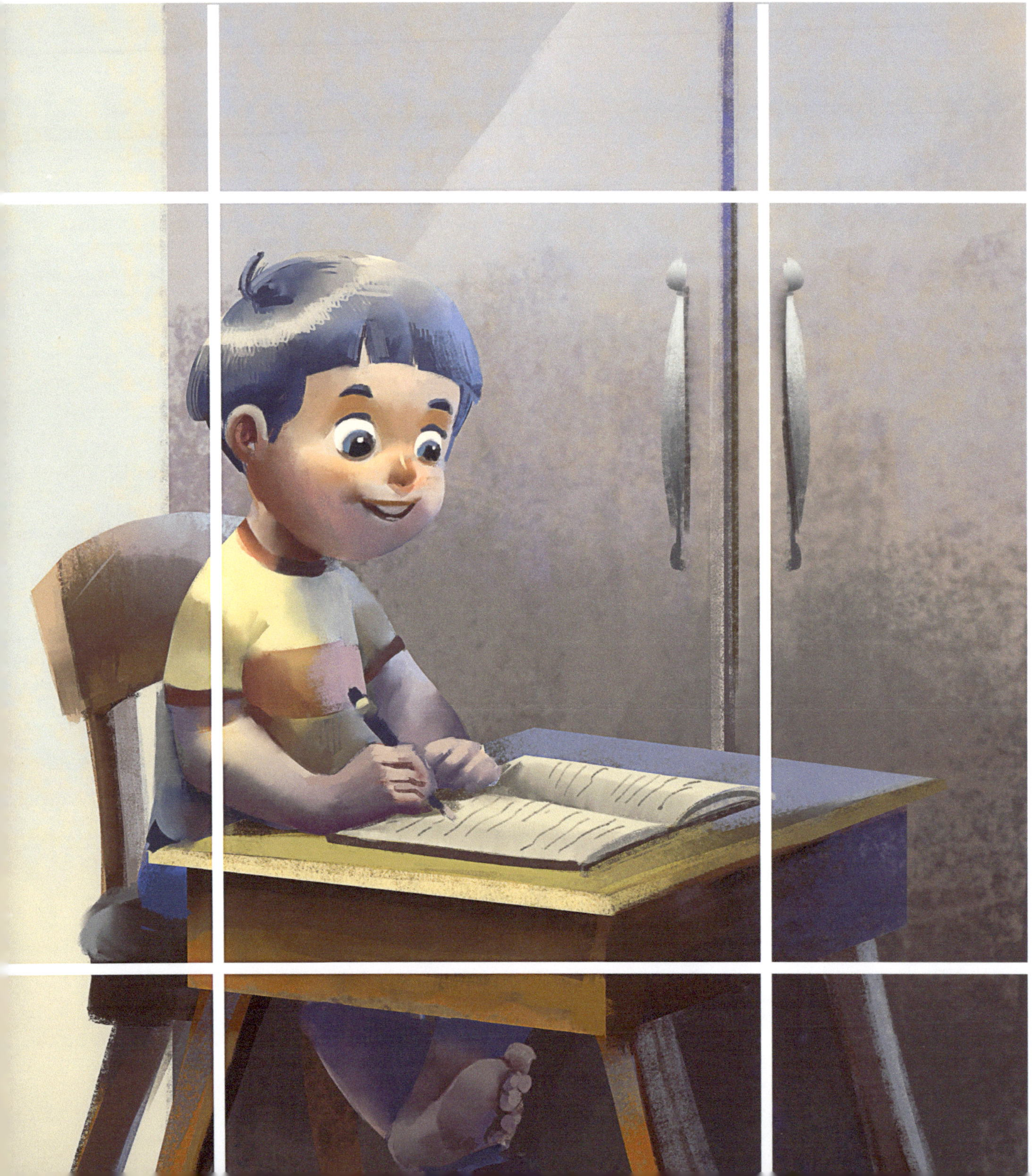

You can write
a happy story,

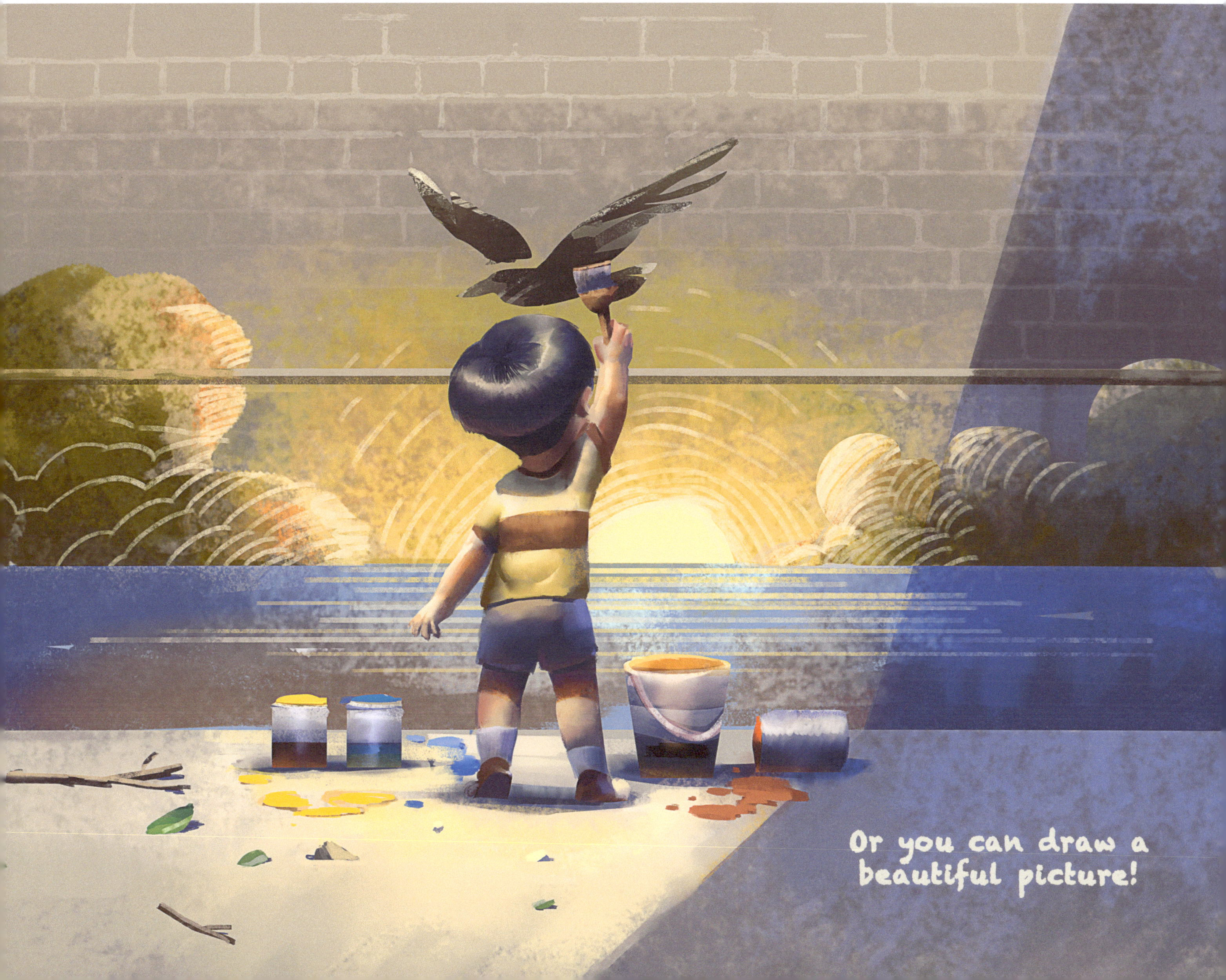

Or you can draw a
beautiful picture!

You can keep some words all ready in your snakebite kit so that you will know what to say if a snake is being mean.

"I don't know if you knew this, but what you just said hurt my feelings". The snake may not have even known that they were being rude! Or maybe they were just having a really bad day.

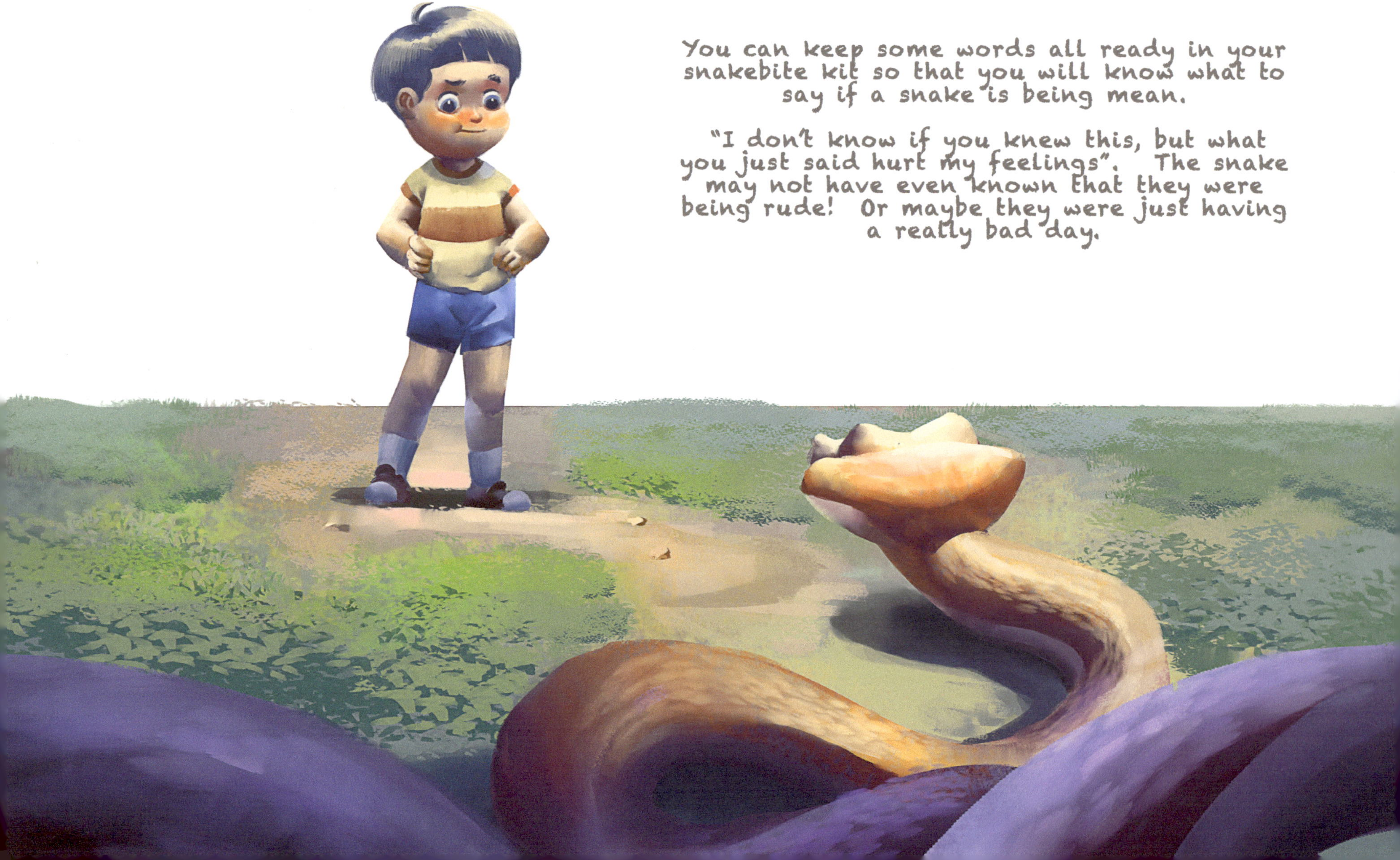

If a snake is being very mean,
or you are scared,
you may need to talk to someone
who can help you and protect you.

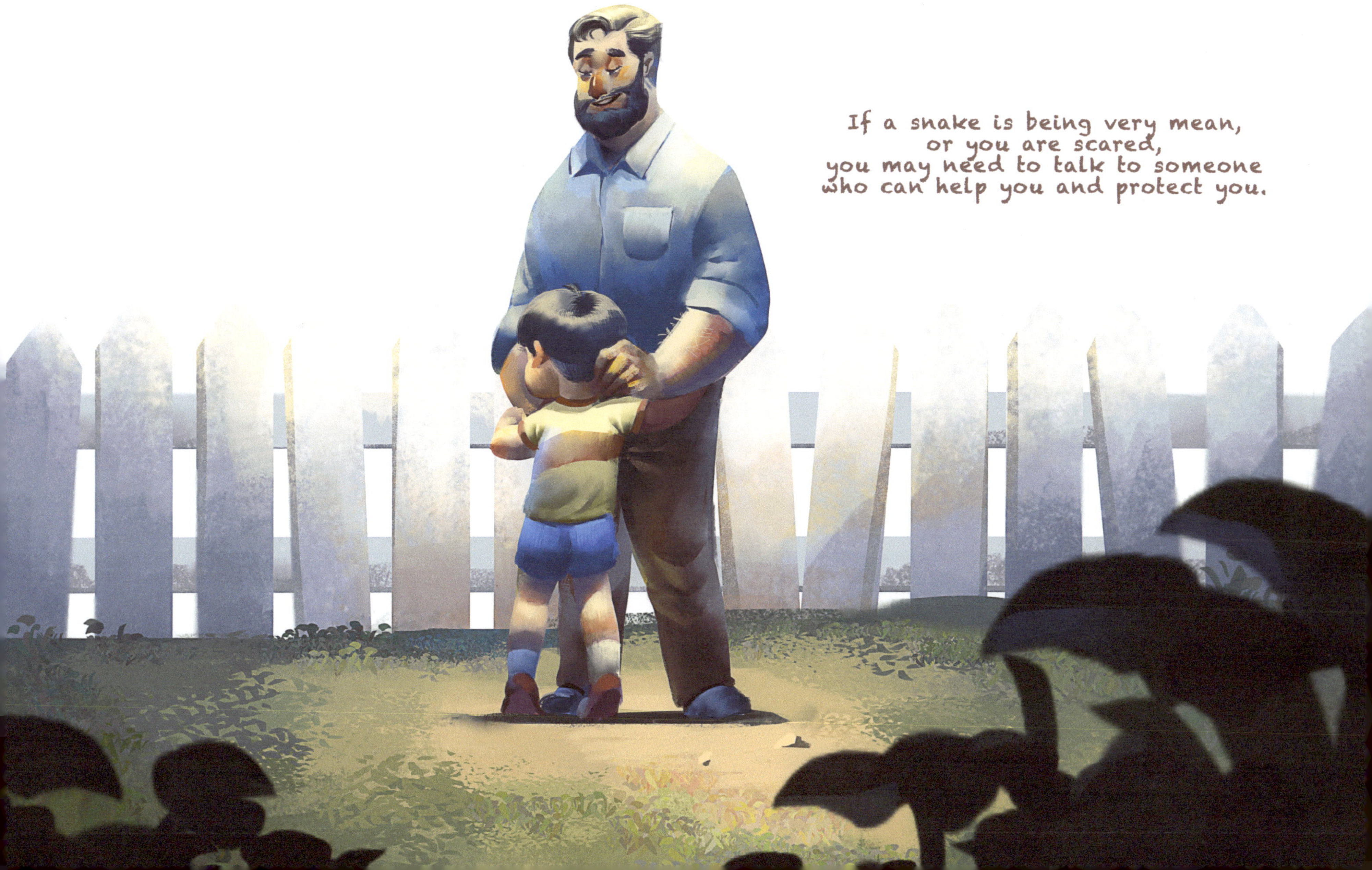

The most important thing to carry in a snakebite kit is a special note, one that reminds you not to say mean things to other people, even if you are having a really bad day.

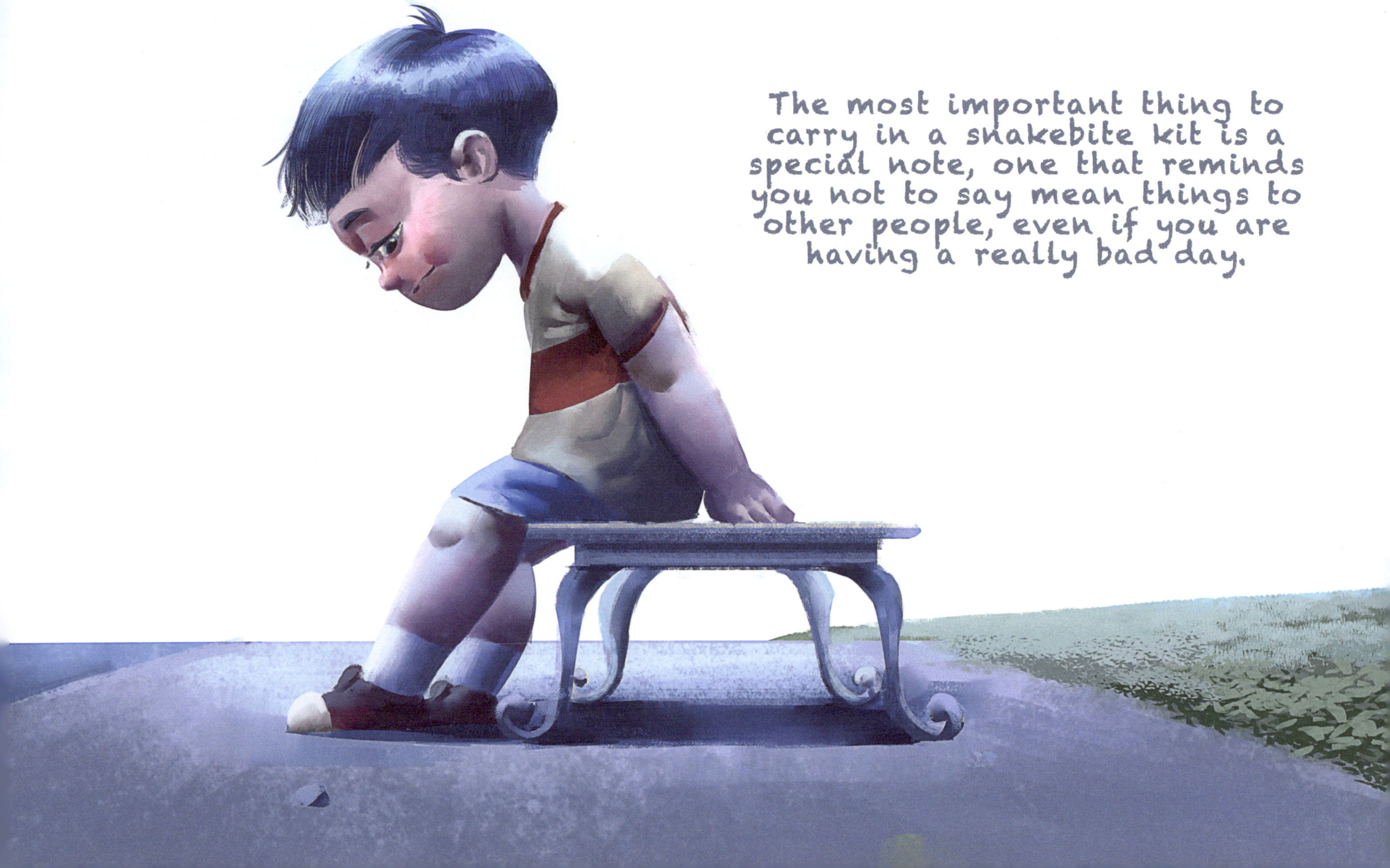

You can share your snakebite kit with others, too! If you see that someone is being picked on by a snake, you can be nice to that person and share ideas from your kit.

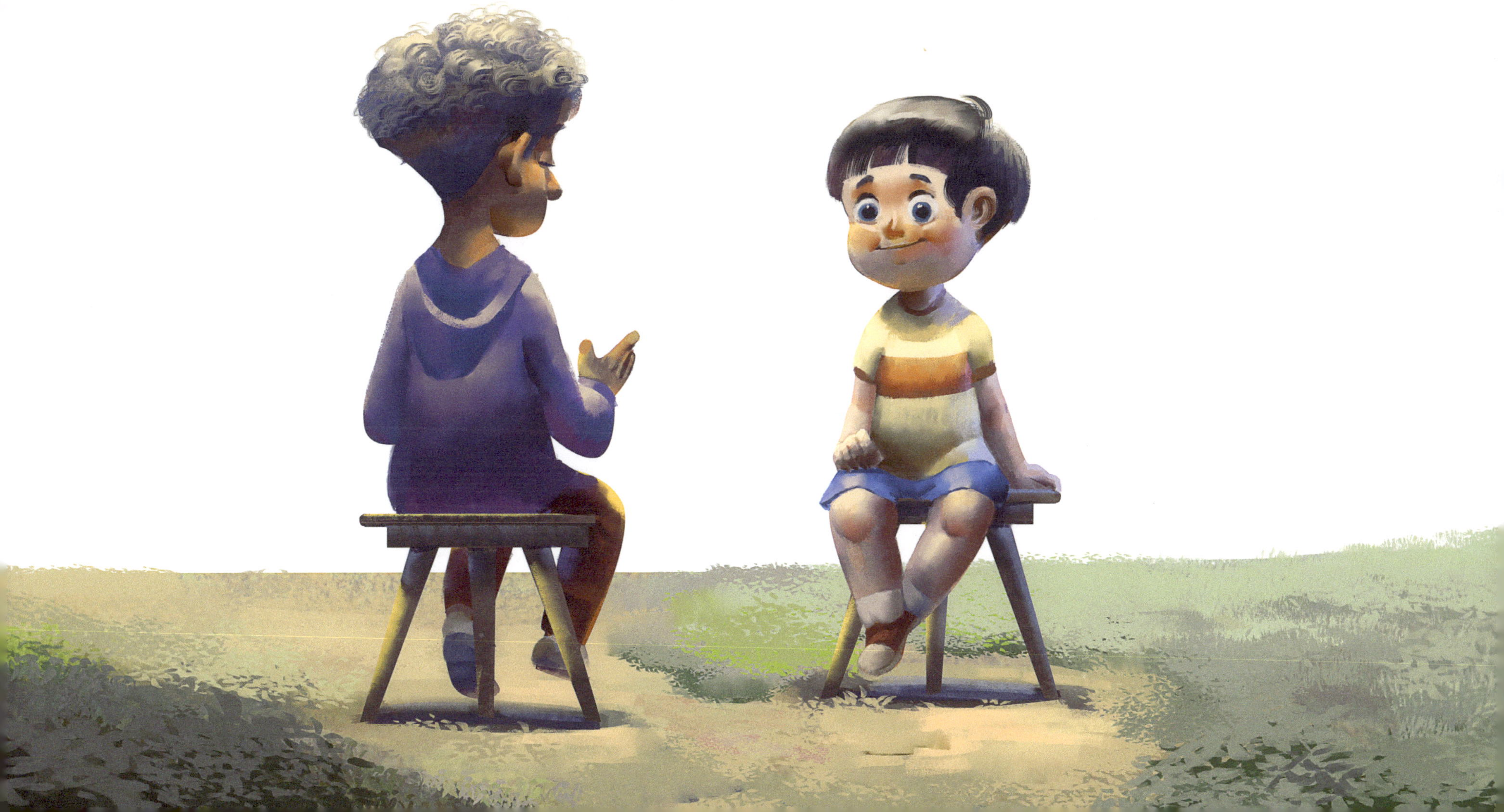

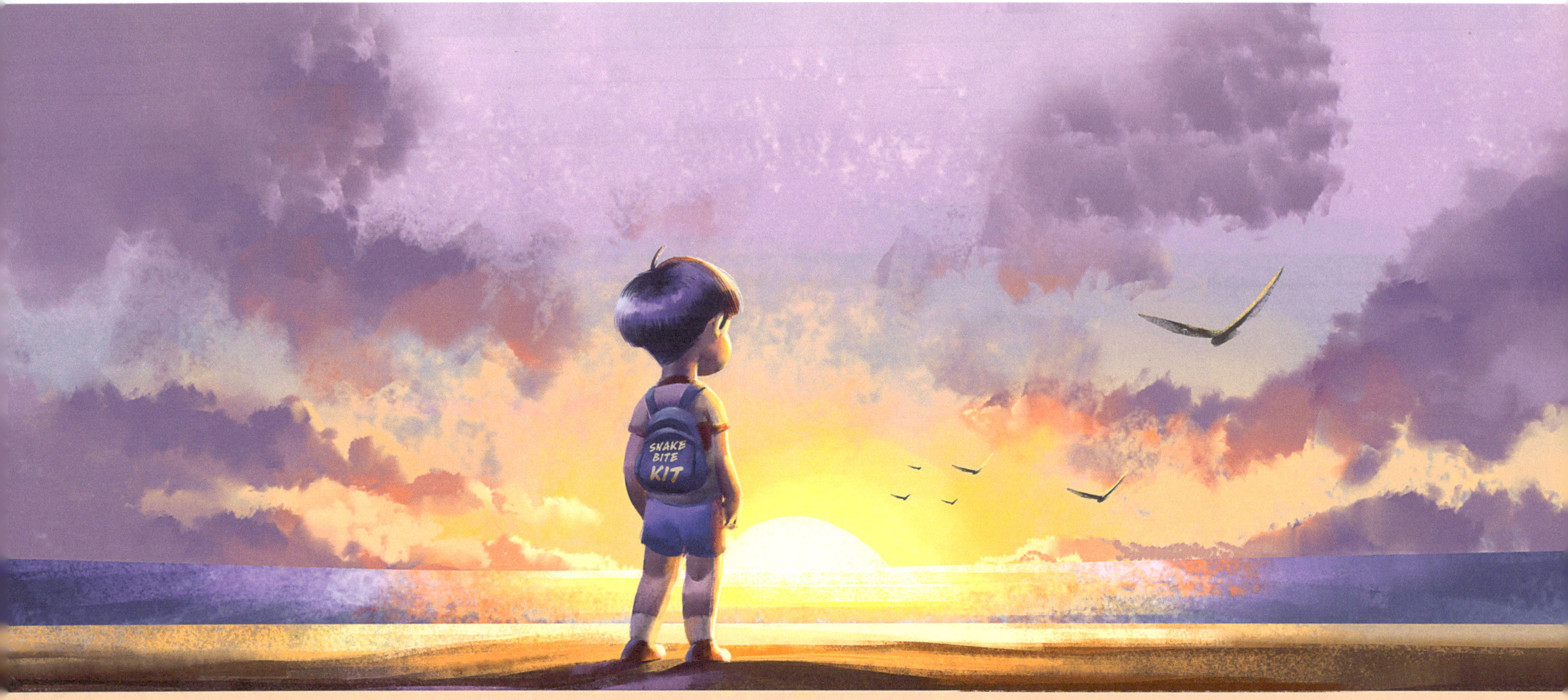
SNAKE
BITE
KIT

There will always be snakes who are mean, and sometimes we can't change that. But there will also always be nice snakes, silly snakes, and snakes that want to help us and be our friends. And who knows, even snakes who are being mean may learn to be nice someday!

Everyone in the world will have a day where someone says something mean to them. Remember, you now have a snakebite kit filled with ideas for dealing with mean words, and you can help yourself, and maybe even help others too!

The End

Printed in the USA
CPSIA information can be obtained
at www.ICGtesting.com
LVHW061030281023
762444LV00037B/319